S0-BDT-021

Samuel Poston

March 28, 2001

Compliments of
The Maiuri Family

JOSEPH L. MULREADY SCHOOL
306 Cox Street
Hudson, MA 01749

ON THE GHOST TRAIL

by Chris Powling

illustrated by Shaunna Peterson

PiCTURE WiNDOW BOOKS
Minneapolis, Minnesota

Editor: Nick Healy
Page Production: Melissa Kes
Art Director: Nathan Gassman
Associate Managing Editor: Christianne Jones

First American edition published in 2007 by
Picture Window Books
5115 Excelsior Boulevard
Suite 232
Minneapolis, MN 55416
877-845-8392
www.picturewindowbooks.com

First published in 2006 by A&C Black Publishers Limited, 38 Soho
Square, London, W1D 3HB, with the title ON THE GHOST TRAIL.

Text copyright © 2006 Chris Powling
Illustrations copyright © 2006 Shaunna Peterson

All rights reserved. No part of this book may be reproduced without
written permission from the publisher. The publisher takes no responsibility
for the use of any of the materials or methods described in this book, nor the
products thereof.

Printed in the United States of America.

Library of Congress Cataloging-in-Publication Data
Powling, Chris.
On the ghost trail / by Chris Powling ; illustrated by Shaunna Peterson.
p. cm. — (Read-it! chapter books)
Summary: After telling his brother and sister that cobwebs are ghost trails,
Adam's practical joke starts to get out of control.
ISBN-13: 978-1-4048-3125-4 (library binding)
ISBN-10: 1-4048-3125-8 (library binding)
[1. Ghosts—Fiction. 2. Practical jokes—Fiction. 3. Brothers and sisters—
Fiction.] I. Peterson, Shaunna, ill. II. Title.
PZ7.P8843On 2006
[Fic]—dc22   2006027268

Table of Contents

Chapter One 5

Chapter Two 13

Chapter Three......................... 19

Chapter Four 32

Chapter Five 41

Chapter One

Grandpa's house is a bit like
Grandpa. It's very old and creaky,
you see. Also, it's rather messy
in a Grandpa-like kind of way.

"My house reminds me of me,"
he always says.

It reminds us of Grandpa, too.
No wonder we love to stay there.
At least we did until our visit last
spring. That's when my big brother,
Adam, started to freak us out.

"Look!" he exclaimed one afternoon. "Do you see all of those cobwebs, Ben?"

"Cobwebs?" I said.

"In the fireplace," Adam said, pointing across the room. "See where the bricks are all sooty? How do you think they got there?"

"Spiders, I suppose," I said.

"No," said Adam. "I don't think so. It wasn't spiders."

"Not spiders?" said Susie, our little sister. "They look like spiderwebs to me."

Adam shook his head. He said, "They may *look* like spiderwebs, Susie. But that's really a ghost trail."

"A ghost trail?" I asked.

"Exactly," he said. "A ghost slipped up the chimney, I suspect. It probably brushed against the brickwork. That web-looking stuff is a little bit of ghost that got left behind."

Susie and I stared at the fireplace. Was it really a ghost trail hanging there? Or were they just ordinary, everyday cobwebs that Grandpa hadn't swept away?

Luckily, Grandpa came in just then with our snack. He noticed right away how quiet we were.

"Anything wrong, kids?" he asked.

"It's Adam," said Susie. "He was telling us—"

"About those cobwebs," Adam cut in.

Grandpa squinted at the fireplace. "Oh dear," he said. "My eyes aren't what they used to be, I'm afraid. This place is getting messy. I hope it won't spoil your appetite."

"Not a chance," said Adam.

After that, we got busy with the snacks. Grandpa joined in, too.

Susie used the new camera she'd gotten for her birthday to take a picture of us all. Everything was back to normal in Grandpa's creaky old house.

Almost normal, anyway.

There was still the ghost trail in the fireplace.

Chapter Two

At bedtime, Adam started teasing us again.

His voice floated down from the top bunk. It was just loud enough for us to hear every word—me in the bunk below him, Susie in her bed over by the window.

"Ben," whispered Adam. "There it is again. Can you hear it?"

"Hear what?" I asked.
"That," said Adam.

Which noise did he mean? At night you can hear lots of noises in a house as old and creaky as Grandpa's.

We could
hear the wind
moaning in the
chimney. We
could hear the
rumble of the
washing machine

downstairs. We could hear the yip
of a fox in the trees out behind
the garden.

But Adam wasn't talking about
these noises.

The noise went TAP, TAP, TAP.

"OK," I said. "What is it?"

"A twig," said Susie. "It's a twig, that's all. Just a twig tapping against the window."

"Yes, it *could* be a twig," said Adam. "It *sounds* like a twig, I agree. Unless it's a ghost's heartbeat, of course."

"A ghost's heartbeat?" I gasped.

"How can it be a ghost's heartbeat?" asked Susie. "A ghost is already dead. It hasn't got a heartbeat anymore."

"Exactly," said Adam. "That's what makes it so scary. It's probably the same ghost that left the trail in the fireplace."

Adam paused, and then he added, "But let's pretend it's just a twig. Good night, Ben! Good night, Susie!"

Then we heard TAP, TAP, TAP again. How could we possibly sleep after that?

Chapter Three

The next day, it was raining hard. We spent the morning curled up with books and newspaper funny pages.

Grandpa's creaky old house had never felt cozier. I almost forgot about the ghost trail. I almost forgot about the ghost's heartbeat, too.

After lunch, the sun came out.

"Leave the cleaning up to me, kids," Grandpa said. "This sunshine may not last. Go outside for a good, brisk walk while you can!"

"Your special path, Grandpa?" asked Susie.

"If you like," Grandpa said. "Can you remember the way?"

We all laughed at that. Grandpa had shown us his special path hundreds of times.

First, we would cross the yard to the hole in his hedge. Then came the long, winding path around the church next door.

After that, we took a shortcut
back through the graveyard until
we arrived at Grandpa's front
door again.

"You'll be safe enough in daylight," Grandpa told us. "There's no need to hurry. Stop for a look and a listen every now and then."

"Exactly!" Adam grinned. "We'll look and listen every step of the way, Grandpa!"

He didn't have to say what for—not after all his teasing yesterday. We'd be looking for ghost trails, that's what. And we'd be listening for ghostly heartbeats, too.

I wanted to say, "No thanks, Adam. You're on your own."

But I kept quiet.

At first, everything was bright and beautiful on Grandpa's special path. I'd never seen Susie take so many pictures.

Of course, I guessed what she was up to. The camera was helping her avoid thoughts of the ghost trail.

I had nothing to distract me. I saw a cobweb dripping with raindrops. "Was it a ghost dressed up for a party?" I thought.

Then I heard the tap, tap, tap of the blossoms against the church porch. "Were a couple of ghosts getting married?" I wondered. Wherever I looked and listened, the springtime seemed full of ghosts.

And it was all Adam's fault.

Susie and I decided to let our big brother go on ahead. Can you blame us for hanging back? At least it meant Susie and I could talk.

"What's wrong with Adam?" I asked her. "Why is he telling us this spooky stuff all of a sudden?"

"What spooky stuff?" asked Susie.

"You know, the cobwebs and tapping and all that," I said. "I suppose you think we should ignore him!"

"Exactly," said Susie.

I was amazed. Honestly, she sounded just like our big brother! Sometimes I can hardly believe she's the baby of the family.

"OK," I said. "But suppose ignoring him doesn't work. What do we do then?"

My little sister scratched her head and thought for a moment. Then she smiled at me.

"We scare him back," said Susie.

Scare him back? We were talking about Adam, weren't we?

He is two years older than I am
and four years older than Susie.
How can you possibly scare your
big brother?

As soon as we caught up with him,
I saw that troubling glint in his eye.

"Midnight," he grinned.

"Midnight?" I asked.

"Midnight tonight, yes. We'll meet here in the graveyard," he said. "We should be here when the church clock is striking 12 midnight. That's the best time to hunt down this ghost of ours. Are you two up for it?"

"Count me out," said Susie. "Who wants to hang around in a graveyard after dark? There's no fun in that. I'd rather be tucked safely in bed, thank you."

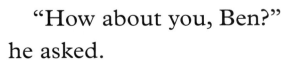

"How about you, Ben?" he asked.

"Me?" I gulped.

"Yes, you," he sighed. "Are you frightened, too?"

Adam looked at me in his most big-brotherly way. He was expecting me to agree with Susie, I think. And that's what I should have done, of course.

I still don't know why I didn't.

Chapter Four

It was nearly midnight. Adam and I slipped quietly out of bed. We dressed without a word. Then we crossed the bedroom on our tiptoes.

Susie didn't say goodbye. I guessed that she was already fast asleep. She didn't stir in her bed when we slowly eased out of the room.

That night, there was no wind at all. There was no rumble from the washing machine, either. The old staircase hardly creaked as we crept downstairs.

Soon we were out in the darkness. Out in the yard, we looked around for foxes.

"Can't see a single one," said my big brother. "They must be taking a night off."

"Lucky foxes," I gulped.

"You scared, Ben?" Adam asked.

"Aren't you?" I asked.

"Nah," he replied.

My big brother sounded scared, though. That should have made me feel better, I suppose. Instead, I was more nervous than ever as we stumbled across the yard. It took us ages to find the gap in the hedge.

"Keep the flashlight still, Adam," I said. "You're making it shine all over the place."

"You hold it then!" he hissed.

"No, not me," I said.

I didn't want to see the ghost first. Maybe Adam didn't, either.

Neither of us had ever seen a night quite like that one. Even the shadows seemed to have a shadow that night—or something pretending to be a shadow ... something as black as a vampire, perhaps ... or as hairy as a werewolf.

"Stay close to me, Ben," said Adam. "We cannot split up, OK?"

"You bet," I said.

The flashlight swung quickly this way and that as we followed the path around the church. Its beam seemed to get weaker and weaker with every step we took. Still, we walked on.

Then, in the middle of the graveyard, the flashlight went out altogether. We stopped in our tracks.

Adam let out a groan.

"The battery is dead!" he said.

"It can't be," I said.

"It is," he replied. "Now I can't see a thing!"

"You're not the only one!" I cried.

We couldn't see anything, but we could still hear—especially when the church clock started to strike.

DONG! DONG! DONG!

Midnight was all around us now.
So were the shadows. It was as if they
were ganging up on us—an ambush
of shadows. Had the darkness been
lying in wait to trip us up? How
would we find our way?

As the last ringing of the bells faded, we both sighed with relief. But the worst wasn't over yet, not by a long shot. Already we could hear another sound.

TAP, TAP, TAP.

I could almost feel how close it was—like the prod of a bony finger. Like the jab of a pointy elbow. Like the beat of a dark heart in a tangle of cobwebs. The sound was forcing me to turn around. Adam was turning around, too.

TAP, TAP, TAP.

There was a bright blast of light.
Luckily, it was too quick to blind us.
It was more like a firework exploding
near your face.

We were shocked, and we ran for
our lives.

Adam barely beat me out of the graveyard. I may have even reached Grandpa's front door ahead of him. I'm not sure. And don't ask me how we scrambled inside without waking up the whole house.

We spent the rest of the night on the sofa downstairs. Neither of us dared go up to bed. Just one creak from that old staircase would have freaked us out.

Chapter Five

That's where Grandpa found us the next morning. He poked his head around the door and winked. "Sleeping on the sofa, eh?" he asked. "Anything to do with last night's little adventure?"

"Adventure?" I said.

"How do you know about that?" Adam asked.

Grandpa tapped his nose.

"I don't miss very much, you know—aside from the odd cobweb here and there," he said. "Do you want to tell me what was going on out there in the dark?"

So we did.

And we didn't just talk about getting stuck in the dark, either. We talked about the ghost trail, too. We even talked about teasing and being teased.

Grandpa nodded his head as he listened. Then he explained that the problem with teasing is knowing when to stop.

"Do you hear what I'm saying, Adam?" Grandpa asked.

"Yes," said Adam, turning red.

"Good," said Grandpa. "There's been a lot of teasing going on around here. Do you have any idea where this came from?"

He held out a photo.

It was a photo printed from Grandpa's computer, and the picture was very clear.

We could see every single detail. We could see the church, the gravestones, and our mouths gaping wide in horror. Midnight was as clear as day in the picture. It always is when you use a flash.

A flash?

So that's what had shocked us—
the flash of a camera.

"Did you take this, Grandpa?"
Adam asked. "Were you following us
all the time?"

"Me?" asked
Grandpa. "At my
age? I'm much too
old and creaky to
chase a couple of
kids around a
graveyard—
especially after
dark. I gave up
that sort of thing
years ago."

Grandpa laughed and added,
"Maybe it was the ghost who caught
you on camera!"

"It must have been a ghost," Adam quickly said.

"Yeah!" I agreed.

After all, who else could it have been? Surely not a kid who is two years younger than I am and four years younger than my brother. No way would that kid be brave enough to follow us into a graveyard in the dead of night.

It's easier to believe in a ghost than in a little sister like that.

Isn't it?

Look for More *Read-it!* Chapter Books

The Badcat Gang
Beastly Basil
Cat Baby
Cleaner Genie
Clever Monkeys
Contest Crazy
Disgusting Denzil
Duperball
Elvis the Squirrel
Eric's Talking Ears
High Five Hank
Hot Dog and the Talent Competition
Nelly the Monstersitter
Scratch and Sniff
Sid and Bolter
Stan the Dog Becomes Superdog
The Thing in the Basement
Tough Ronald

Looking for a specific title? A complete list
of *Read-it!* Chapter Books is available on our Web site:
www.picturewindowbooks.com